# CLIFFHOUSE FOOTPRINTS

## SUNRISE ISLAND SERIES PREQUEL

## MAREN HILL

ISBN 978-1-7388658-2-6

Published by Sandpiper Press

Cover design by Sleepy Fox Studios

Cover Images copyright Shutterstock

Sandpiper Press

www.marenhill.com

https://www.amazon.com/stores/Maren-Hill/author/B09TPY8G6T

 Formatted with Vellum

*For all who value the meaning of motherhood.*

# TRIGGER WARNING

This story contains a brief depiction of a child going missing from school. While this incident serves to highlight the strong bond between caregiver and child, readers who may be sensitive to themes involving missing children are advised to approach with caution.

# 1

---



*1970, Sunrise Island, B.C.*

"**G**ood morning." John's baritone voice carried through the farmhouse kitchen as he answered the bright yellow push-button wall phone.

Morning light spilled across the worn wooden table, catching on a chipped mug and the folded newspaper he hadn't yet opened.

On the other end, Shirley hesitated—just long enough for him to notice. The warmth in her voice was still there, but something else had slipped in. Something unsteady.

"Hey, Shirl, everything okay?"

Silence stretched between them long enough for John to shift his weight, his gaze drifting toward the window.

"John...I—I need to tell you something."

The words lingered, fragile and unfinished, as he waited.

With a trembling voice, Shirley shared the more hopeful aspect of her stage-two breast cancer diagnosis. "With the right treatment, they say it can be cured—with a low chance of it coming back."

John stood motionless, his breath shallow as he absorbed her words.

When he finally spoke, his voice was steady, grounded. "You're only twenty-nine, Shirl. And you've always been healthy. You've got a good chance of beating this."

"That's what the doctors say," she replied, a quiet exhale following.

He tightened his grip on the receiver. "Why don't you come to the farm for a while? Bring Michael. It might do you both some good."

He looked out toward the far field. "I can show him the spring lambs. They're all over the island right now."

JOHN AND KATHLEEN WERE PREPARED. Kathleen had baked an apple pie from their own apples, harvested the previous fall, and there was plenty of ice cream in the freezer. John planned to take Michael for a horse-and-buggy ride, giving Kathleen and Shirley time to talk.

Rising from their veranda chairs, Kathleen and John made their way toward the circular driveway where Shirley had parked her car. As they reached the passenger door, Kathleen smiled warmly at Michael.

"Well, look at you—all grown up," she said, her voice full of affection. "Eight already! Time flies."

Michael grinned up at her, his hazel eyes bright. "Hi, Aunt Kathleen," he said, a little shy, his hands tucked into his pockets.

Kathleen opened the door and helped him out. "Come here, you," she said, pulling him into a tight hug. "You're looking more like your dad every day—you know that?"

Michael didn't answer, but he smiled faintly as he hugged her back.

When she let him go, her voice softened. "We've got apple pie waiting, and your Uncle John has a horse-and-buggy ride planned. How does that sound?"

"Awesome!" Michael's face lit up at the mention of the ride.

Kathleen gave him one last squeeze before stepping back. "Go on and get settled. We'll take good care of your mom."

JOHN'S SHETLAND PONY, Frisky, trotted down the driveway, pulling a two-wheeled cart. Seated beside his Uncle John, Michael grinned, practically bouncing with excitement. He waved to his mother, Shirley, and his aunt, Kathleen, watching from the farmhouse veranda.

Kathleen, still lithe and sprightly after her retirement as Head Gardener at Butchart's, smiled at Michael's enthusiasm. She turned to Shirley. "Why don't you come sit with me for a bit?" she suggested in a light, sing-song voice, motioning to the cushioned wicker chair beside her. "I've got some tea ready."

Shirley, her complexion pale and eyes tired, offered a faint smile as she sank into the chair, her gaze distant. She took a sip of her tea but set the cup down quickly, the clink of porcelain against the saucer echoing her unease. Kathleen, sensing her sister-in-law's anxiety, didn't bother with small talk. She waited, letting the silence stretch, until Shirley finally spoke.

"Look," Shirley said, her voice firm, "if I'm going to beat this, I can't afford to hold anything back. I need to give it everything."

Kathleen nodded, her heart heavy. "Do they know how long it'll take, Shirley—the treatment and recovery?"

Shirley sighed. "Radiation alone is six weeks, then chemo, and who knows what else along the way," she said. Her voice was steady, but the strain had taken its toll.

Kathleen's mind spun with concern. "And recovery?" she asked, her words gentle, her eyes searching Shirley's face.

"Three months. Maybe more. They said anywhere between three to eighteen months, depending on how everything goes," Shirley replied, her voice cracking slightly.

Kathleen absorbed the timeline in stunned silence. *It could take up to eighteen months.*

She turned to Shirley, her voice soft but edged with concern. "Who'll care for Michael while you're going through this?"

Shirley's gaze wandered, the trill of a red-winged blackbird breaking the silence. Kathleen reached out, her hand resting lightly over Shirley's, sensing the depth of her despair.

"There's no one else, Kathleen," Shirley whispered, her voice thick with emotion. "John's the only family I have here."

Kathleen's mind raced, searching for alternatives. She remembered that Mark, Shirley's late husband, had come from a Dutch family. "What about Mark's family? Do they still live in Holland?"

Shirley nodded. "Yes. After Mark passed, his brother Dan talked about coming over, but it never happened."

Kathleen squeezed Shirley's hand, offering a gentle smile. "Would you like another cup of tea, Shirl?" she asked, hoping to shift the mood and give herself a moment to think.

"Yes, sure," Shirley murmured, her tone softer now. Her shoulders slumped a little as she gazed toward the garden. "I don't know how I'll manage all this, Kathleen," she whispered.

Kathleen gave Shirley's hand a reassuring touch, her heart aching for her sister-in-law. "We'll figure it out, Shirl," she said gently with a soft smile.

"I hope you're right," Shirley murmured.

Kathleen's words were steady and firm. "We're in this together, honey. We'll do everything we can to help."

IN THE KITCHEN, Kathleen kept thinking about Shirley. She knew in her heart that she and John would step up, no matter what. She opened the kitchen door and walked out across the field toward the clifftop, hoping to clear her head. By the time she returned to the veranda, she was certain of what needed to be done.

"We'll take care of Michael while you focus on getting better, Shirl," she said, her voice firm but warm. "You don't even have to ask."

Shirley didn't speak but reached for Kathleen, tears streaming down her face as they embraced. Kathleen held her tighter, feeling Shirley's body tremble against hers as she released pent-up sobs that broke Kathleen's heart.

**2**

———————

*Eight Months Earlier*

On a balmy July evening, the fragrance of summer jasmine lingered in the air, lending a quiet sensuality. Kathleen cherished this hour of the day, when the chores were finished, and she and John eased into their favourite chairs on the veranda, simply enjoying each other's company. Henley, her calico cat, purred contentedly on the sun-warmed floorboards, the sound blending with the distant murmur of the sea in a quiet, steady rhythm.

As the sun dipped below the horizon, the sky melted into warm shades of amber and rose, and twilight settled over the veranda like a gentle hush. Sweethearts since childhood, they basked in that familiar ease between them—the comfort of shared history and the quiet intimacy of long years together.

Kathleen cast a sidelong look toward John. "There's something about the air on a night like this, isn't there, love?"

After supper, she had luxuriated in a vanilla-scented bubble bath in their deep soaker tub, a glass of white wine cool against her lips. The water droplets glistened delicately on the surface of her fair skin, like scattered jewels reflecting the soft ambient light. Even at 31, Kathleen was a canvas of natural beauty with high cheekbones and grey-green eyes. Her hair had a soft, buttery hue, flowing down her back like silk and framing her face with alluring elegance.

She slipped a silky, barely-there pink dress over her head, the spaghetti straps showcasing the purity of her freshly cleansed skin. A memory surfaced—John's teasing words from the first time they'd made love: "What do you do, take a milk bath every day?

John's six-foot-one frame made the teak lounger seem smaller than it was. Even though he was still strong and fit, John's physique was no longer as refined as it used to be. He liked to think he was still eligible for combat despite a noticeable limp and an honourable discharge. He kept his hair short and his face clean-shaven, just how Kathleen liked it, and still got up at 5:30 a.m., ready for action.

He shifted slightly, a silent invitation for her to come inside, where the warmth of their home—and each other—awaited.

JOHN AND KATHLEEN had always longed for children of their own. Back when Kathleen lived in Central Saanich and worked at Butchart Gardens, she embraced the role of auntie to her cousin Maggie's children, Robert and Natalie. Though technically her second cousins, Maggie encouraged them to see Kathleen as their aunt—a reflection of the lifelong bond between the two women.

Kathleen showered the children with affection, but it only deepened the quiet ache within her. She found a natural rhythm in caring for them, a sense of purpose that felt both joyful and incomplete.

For both John and Kathleen, building a family was more

than a dream—it was something they felt deeply, a longing to fill their home with life, connection, and the kind of memories that would endure.

Kathleen also carried a fierce sense of responsibility for her heritage property, which had been in her family since 1910. When Kathleen's father, Robert, passed away the year she and John were married, she inherited a sprawling home on a thousand acres.

Determined to preserve that legacy, she made it clear in her will that the farm was to remain in the family for as long as possible. If circumstances changed in the future, it was to be entrusted to the Heritage Society of Sunrise Island.

Kathleen could still remember cradling newborn Robert in her arms, his tiny body filling her with awe. The rhythmic rise and fall of his breath, the soft movements of his body, stirred something deep and instinctive—a need to protect, to nurture, to hold on. His closed eyes and curled fingers, so vulnerable and fragile, only deepened that pull.

Bathing Natalie, she savoured the delicate fragrance of her newborn skin—that fleeting mix of warmth and sweetness unlike anything she had ever known. *I have to have one of my own.*

The eldest of five siblings, John understood the fullness—and chaos—of a big family. "It was like living in a bustling village," John once told her, "all under one roof."

With his siblings scattered all over the world and his sister, Shirley, living in Canada, he held that connection close. Shirley and Michael visited the farm often, just a thirty-five-minute ferry ride from their home near Victoria.

ON A CHILLY SEPTEMBER MORNING, a gentle breeze carried the

crisp scent of Ambrosia apples through the orchard. John took in their sprawling land, appreciation shining in his eyes.

"We have plenty of room to raise a big family, Kath... if we're lucky." He turned, giving her a playful wink, and she smiled, sharing the same quiet hope.

"Now that we're both retired, love, this feels like the perfect time to start a family," Kathleen said.

John and Kathleen had been childhood sweethearts, and he had proposed just before his deployment overseas. As much as she loved him, Kathleen had turned him down, knowing she wasn't cut out to be a military wife. She knew her own mind, and not even love could change it.

**3**

———————

Dr. Chalmers gave Kathleen a gentle smile as she stepped into the small examination room. "Not this time, I'm afraid," she said softly.

Kathleen's heart sank. She was weary of hearing the same disappointing news and had hoped this time would mark the beginning of a new chapter.

Dr. Chalmers gave her a reassuring look. "You and John are healthy. Sometimes, it just takes time. I have patients who waited nearly ten years before conceiving."

Kathleen's shoulders slumped as she sighed deeply. "Dr. Chalmers, I won't be one of those. I set a limit of two years, and that limit is up. Call me impatient if you want, but that's the way I am." She shrugged, her hands falling limply into her lap. "I just have to accept that it's not happening."

Dr. Chalmers stepped aside and asked, "Have you considered adoption?"

Kathleen's voice was firm. "No. I want to have my own baby, of my own blood. Adoption isn't the picture I've held in my head ever since I was a young girl."

After a moment, her expression softened. "Thanks. I'll think about it, but at this stage, I can't see it." She stood, offering Dr. Chalmers a faint smile before turning to leave.

The door clicked softly behind her as she stepped out into the corridor. For a moment, she stood still, gathering herself, the familiar weight of disappointment settling deeper than she wanted to admit.

John was waiting.

He looked up the moment she appeared.

And in that quiet instant between them, before either of them spoke, he already knew.

As Kathleen and John drove up their long gravel driveway and parked in the turnaround, Kathleen's eyes swept across their expansive heritage farm. The flower gardens were alive with vibrant blooms, and the fruit orchards were preparing to release their bounty later in the season. She imagined their child playing in a cornfield maze, learning to ride a pony, and sailing a model boat on the milldam.

Instead of going into the house, Kathleen strolled past the barn and the corral, heading toward the clifftop. Perched on the low-lying limb of an arbutus tree, she delved into the deepest recesses of her mind, grappling with the heavy legacy left by her father and the generations before him. The expectation that the Mitchell estate would remain within the family line pressed down on her like a crushing force. Kathleen feared that if she and John couldn't conceive—or if they turned to adoption—the family records would read "no issue" next to their names, a label that would haunt her.

Kathleen's thoughts churned. *If I don't get pregnant, the direct bloodline ends with me. And if we adopt, our family legacy continues with someone who's not of our blood.*

Considering the possibilities, Kathleen realized that adoption could offer her the chance to be a mom, even if in a different form. She'd still experience all the ups and downs that come with raising a child. Adoption, she figured, could satisfy her deep yearning for motherhood and keep the family legacy alive—blood ties aside. Besides, raising a child together would only bring her and John closer. Natalie and Robert would get a second cousin, and Maggie a first.

Kathleen smiled with satisfaction as she kicked a pile of crispy arbutus leaves into the air.

Leaning back on the outstretched limb, Kathleen gazed at the sun's dazzling display across the strait. Her thoughts drifted to a future where an adopted child could blend seamlessly into the fabric of their family—much like John, who had become an integral part of the Mitchell family even though his biological family name was Milton.

Still, a subtle undercurrent of sentimentality held Kathleen in its grip, a yearning for a grandchild who would carry the unmistakable imprint of Mitchell's DNA—a connection to the past and a bridge to the future. But the more she reflected on her dilemma, the more it became clear to her that the expectations she felt bound to uphold were tied to an age-old belief, one that perhaps no longer held relevance in today's world.

## 4

As she reflected on the past two years of trying to conceive with John, their pursuit seemed more elusive than ever. Dr. Chalmer's suggestion lingered in Kathleen's mind, refusing to be dismissed.

During a quiet moment over coffee on the veranda, she finally brought up adoption. "Is that something you'd be interested in, John?" Her voice was calm, an invitation to something that could reshape their lives. For a moment, it felt as though the space between them held still.

Pausing his watering before the day's heat set in, John considered Kathleen's question. He rubbed his chin, his expression thoughtful. "Not something I'd considered, hon. But, you know, it's not a bad idea. I'd have to give it more thought." His right knee bounced with nervous energy, a telltale sign of his uncertainty.

"Yes, we'd want to be sure," Kathleen added. "I've been thinking about it since Dr. Chalmers brought it up, and the more I consider it, the more appealing it becomes."

John's bouncing knee gradually slowed as if his body were making space for the thoughts unfolding in his mind. In the quiet of the veranda, he turned to Kathleen and asked, 'What is it that appeals to you about it, hon?"

Having fully mulled over the topic, Kathleen didn't hesitate. "To me, a baby is a baby. Sure, it wouldn't be our blood, but I wonder how much that matters in the end. If you raise a child from the very start, surely they become your own."

"I imagine so," John replied softly, his voice thoughtful as he turned her words over in his mind.

Kathleen remained resolute. "You know how much I value family, dear, and my maternal instincts are very strong. I know that from being with Natalie and Robert from the time they were born."

John winked at her and smiled, acknowledging her sentiment.

"Plus," she continued, "and you will laugh at the repetition, I desperately want to preserve the family legacy."

John chuckled, knowing how much Kathleen valued the family legacy. He raised another point. "What about your cousin, Maggie?"

Kathleen nodded. "True, there's Maggie and her kids. The bloodline will carry on—for now, anyway. Who knows if they'll care about Sunrise Island? It's not for everyone."

Kathleen's unease was clear as she turned the situation over in her mind. "The way things stand, John, I don't have a new generation to pass anything to. I want to change that before it's too late," she said, her voice conveying a sense of urgency.

John stayed quiet, letting her finish her thoughts without interruption.

When Kathleen made up her mind, it was as steady and unwavering as an ancient Western Red Cedar. After a long pause, she gave her final answer. "For me, my love," Kathleen said, her voice firm, "it comes down to this: a child is a child, and a mother is a mother, no matter the bloodlines. So if you're willing to adopt, I'll call the agency right now."

**5**

———

"**E**veryone wants a newborn," the weary female voice on the other end of the line replied. "You could be waiting years, to be honest, before one becomes available."

Kathleen's spirits sank, a queasiness settling in her stomach. She had assumed the adoption process would be more straightforward, and she hadn't realized how scarce infants were.

"We do have plenty of older children in need of loving homes," the adoption agency representative continued. "For instance, we're currently seeking a stable environment for a ten-year-old boy. His journey has been tumultuous following the tragic loss of his parents."

As Kathleen listened, her heart ached for the boy, imagining the hardships he had endured from such a young age. She couldn't fathom what he'd already survived. Her thoughts were consumed by a quiet hope for his future, wishing that he would find the happiness and stability every child deserves.

"If you're still interested, you can complete the application. The wait time is usually two to three years."

**6**

*pril 8, 1970*

As Shirley pulled up to park in the circular drive-way, Kathleen watched Michael through the window, his expression a mix of excitement and apprehension.

Stepping off the veranda, Kathleen and John welcomed their eight-year-old nephew to Cliffhouse Farm in a new way, and Kathleen sensed a shift in Michael's perception. She realized that the idyllic world where he'd always felt cherished and adored by his Uncle John and Auntie Kathleen might no longer hold the same magic for him.

John held the car door as Michael stepped out, clutching his small suitcase tightly, his gaze lingering on his mother. Kathleen imagined Shirley's smile was bittersweet, weighed down by the inevitability of their impending separation.

Shirley had believed this would be easier—easier than staying at the farm with Michael, putting him to bed, and then not being there in the morning. But in the end, she realized there was no easy way.

As Shirley and Michael exchanged a prolonged hug, she promised, "I'll call you tonight before you go to bed and give you my goodnight kiss, like we always do, okay, Bud?" Her voice wavered slightly, her attempt to hide her sadness clear.

"Okay, Mom," Michael said quietly, his attention shifting as Kathleen and John stepped out onto the veranda. Their welcoming smiles offered a glimmer of comfort amid the difficult goodbye.

Kathleen leaned in, wrapping her arms around Michael in a warm embrace. Her presence was like a quiet reassurance, offering him a steady sense of comfort amid the uncertainty.

John knelt on the grass with open arms, a playful invitation for Michael to join him. With a gleeful grin, Michael sprinted into his uncle's embrace, the warmth of familial love wrapping around them in a moment of pure joy as his laughter echoed across the lawn.

Kathleen felt a spark of renewed hope as she watched, believing that she and John could work together to restore the sense of boundless adventure and joyful innocence that had always defined Michael's visits to the farm.

But deep down, she knew it wouldn't be that simple.

**7**

———

Kathleen helped settle Michael into the bedroom where he'd slept since he was three. Shirley had handed over a box filled with some of his favorite things to help make his room feel like home. Together, Kathleen and Michael carefully arranged his treasures: a huge box of colorful Legos, a golden yellow Tonka dump truck, a Magic 8-Ball, and a View-Master with a stack of cardboard discs featuring *Star Trek*.

Just as promised, Shirley called Michael at 7 p.m. that evening. John and Kathleen stepped out of the kitchen, giving him some privacy, though they remained within earshot.

"Mom," Michael said tearfully, skipping the usual greeting. "You forgot my G.I. Joe."

"Oh, dear," Kathleen whispered to John, surprised that the toy soldier meant so much to him.

John's eyes met a knowing glance from Kathleen, as if hinting at something she hadn't considered. "Yeah, I know he wanted to bring his G.I. Joe because he knows I used to be a soldier," he said, his tone carrying a hint of disappointment.

"Look at us," Kathleen chuckled. Already getting swept up

in Michael's emotions, she added, half-joking, "Do you think it'll be a rollercoaster ride the whole time he's with us?"

"Let's hope so," John grinned. "That little guy sure knows how to tug at our heartstrings when he's not completely happy. We might wear ourselves out trying to keep him content if we're not careful."

"Agreed, dear. Let's just say we've got a lot to learn about raising kids..." Kathleen's voice trailed off as she reminded herself that Michael wasn't their child. They were his temporary caregivers, not his parents.

BY EIGHT O'CLOCK, Michael was tucked into bed, having listened to Kathleen read just a few pages of *Fantastic Mr. Fox* before drifting off to sleep. That was after she'd checked under the bed, behind the curtains, and in the closet, reassuring him that no scary creatures were hiding in the room.

**8**

———

Kathleen smiled to herself. After immersing in books about child-rearing, anticipating the possibility of one day having a baby of their own, she had come to understand the importance of involving children in household tasks. Life at the farm offered countless opportunities for shared work throughout the seasons.

By the time they gathered for breakfast after Michael's successful first overnight alone, Kathleen felt a deep sense of satisfaction. She was pleased with the plan she had developed to show Michael how he could contribute to the family chores and responsibilities. She intended to start right after breakfast. She chuckled to herself, pleased with the thought that she wouldn't give him the chance to get bored.

Starting with the enjoyable tasks, she planned to show him how to collect the eggs and brush the goats. Grateful that Michael had come to live at the farm in April when there was so much to do outdoors, she wanted him to feel at home before starting Grade 3 at Chickadee Elementary in Ganges.

"Would you like pancakes for breakfast, Michael?" Kathleen asked, believing that good food makes everything better.

Michael's eyes lit up. "Yum," he replied. "And can we have maple syrup?"

"It wouldn't be pancakes without maple syrup," she said, blending wet ingredients into dry and giving the batter a quick stir. Kathleen's apple pancakes had been a favourite for years.

The screen door swung open, and John entered, leaving his work boots outside. He enveloped Kathleen and then Michael in a warm hug. Loving gestures were a regular part of life at Cliffhouse, and John and Kathleen believed they'd help Michael settle in.

"I'm taking a break from woodworking to share some real maple syrup with my two favourite people," John said, sitting at the kitchen table. "By the way," he asked, eager to teach his nephew new skills, "Have you ever used a hammer, Michael?"

Meanwhile, Michael studied Kathleen as she expertly removed six large, fluffy pancakes and six pieces of crispy bacon from the grill, serving two per person. She placed the jar of maple syrup in front of Michael, noting how his eyes widened at the spread before him. A brief, wordless exchange of glances between John and Kathleen suggested that John's question would be set aside for now.

Kathleen barely contained her joy as she watched Michael settle at the kitchen table. Not wanting to make him self-conscious, she resisted the urge to stare, but she appreciated the privilege of watching him grow over the next year. She imagined the boy before her blossoming into a young man, and though he would eventually return to his mother's home, she looked forward to seeing how he'd change and develop in the years to come.

"Listen," Kathleen said, raising her brows and widening her eyes. "Do you hear the hens cackling, Michael? That means they're laying eggs right now."

Michael paused, a forkful of pancake hovering. "Yeah," he said, grinning, shifting excitedly in his chair. "Let's go out right after I eat, okay, Auntie?" The way Michael said "Auntie" melted Kathleen's heart every time.

AFTER BREAKFAST, Kathleen fetched the wire egg basket from the pantry and lined it with a clean, red dish towel. "This is what we use to gather the eggs, Michael. The dish towel will help keep the eggs separated so they don't hit each other and break."

As they strolled down the wood chip trail toward the henhouse, Kathleen noticed a wide grin stretching across Michael's face. The early morning sunlight cast a warm glow on his tousled hair, and his cheeks flushed with excitement. With a determined stride, he moved forward, his enthusiasm evident with each step.

As they approached the henhouse, Kathleen emphasized the importance of maintaining cleanliness in the henhouse and yard. Swinging open the henhouse door, she noticed the six nesting boxes were empty, except for the one in the middle. "Hmm," she said, smiling, "we usually like to gather eggs when the hen isn't in the nest." They walked quietly across the straw-strewn floor toward the nesting boxes.

With his small hands firmly gripping the wire basket, Michael scanned the coop as two of the remaining hens awkwardly scurried out the small door leading to the fenced-in yard. Kathleen gently coaxed the one remaining hen that refused to budge. "They usually leave the nest at feeding time, but this broody hen seems determined to stay here. "Come on, little one, go join your friends."

"Look at that, Michael. They've left us a good number of eggs this morning."

Michael carefully examined the eggs nestled in the boxes.

"That one's blue," he declared, glancing at Kathleen as if seeking confirmation.

"I know," Kathleen replied. "Sometimes, when eggs aren't store-bought, you'll notice blue ones. It all comes down to how the hens are raised—their diet and where they live make all the difference."

"On Mitchell Farm, our eggs come in three colors: white, brown, and blue. Now, why don't you start with this first box? Remember, the eggs are very delicate, so please handle them gently, one at a time, dear, to avoid any breakage."

Kathleen watched with delight as Michael reached for a large brown egg—one of four in the first nest box—and carefully placed it in the wire basket.

"That's it," she smiled. "Now, one more thing. When you add the next egg, try to keep it from touching the first one, if you can. I know it isn't always possible."

Michael followed Kathleen's instructions diligently. As he arranged the eggs in the basket, he made sure they didn't touch each other. With each egg he placed, his eyes lit up as he cradled the warm treasure in his palm.

As he added the second layer, she cautioned him to be extra careful. "Adding layers increases the weight on the eggs below, so we never stack more than five layers in the basket to avoid breakage."

With each successful addition, Michael's grin widened, radiating a sense of accomplishment.

Michael's chest swelled with quiet pride as he moved along the boxes, collecting 11 eggs from the first three. Kathleen, pleased with her choice of a simple yet meaningful task, hoped it would help nurture his sense of responsibility and deepen their bond. She wanted him to understand the value of working together as a family.

When they reached the box where the broody hen still

nestled, Kathleen stepped in. "I'll reach under this red hen if she'll let me."

The hen squawked in protest as Kathleen swiftly dipped her hand under the hen and into the nest, feeling the warmth of the freshly laid eggs. Spotting the newly laid treasure, Michael reached for the egg closest to him, but the indignant hen pecked his hand, causing him to recoil.

"Ouch!" he exclaimed, dropping the egg basket with a thud.

"Oh, I'm sorry, honey; are you okay?" Kathleen called as she turned to watch Michael race out of the henhouse door without looking back. Retrieving the basket from the straw-strewn floor, Kathleen could already see a few egg drippings seeping over the straw. Although she would clean up the mess later, her priority was to tend to Michael.

"Michael," she called out as she headed back up the trail. Not finding him nearby, she went into the kitchen and set the dripping basket in the sink. She called for him throughout the house—both upstairs and downstairs—but received no response.

Growing concerned, Kathleen stepped outside again, scanning for any sign of Michael. She moved briskly around the farmhouse perimeter, checking behind bushes and around corners, but he was nowhere to be seen. Panic began to creep in as she realized he must have wandered off somewhere on their thousand-acre property.

"He's in here!" John shouted from the open barn door. Relieved, she slowed down and headed toward the barn, taking a deep breath to steady herself. She knew that how she handled the situation would shape Michael's memory of their time together on the farm.

"He ran in here, looking upset," John said with a half-smile. "But I couldn't get him to say what happened."

Kathleen sighed. "Aw, it was just unlucky, dear. That broody, red hen pecked his little hand when he reached for an egg. It's all my fault."

In the dim barn, Kathleen saw Michael sitting on a bale of hay, cradling his hand to his chest. "Hey there, buddy," she said softly, trying to catch his eye. "Are you okay?"

Stepping closer, Kathleen crouched down to meet Michael at eye level and offered him a comforting smile. "I'm sorry that happened, sweetheart," she said gently. "Sometimes, animals get protective of their nests, just as people can be protective of what they cherish."

She paused, allowing Michael a moment to absorb her words.

Michael folded his arms. "Humph," he replied angrily, "I'm never going back into that stupid henhouse again."

Michael looked up, his eyes red-rimmed and welling with tears. "She pecked me," he mumbled, his voice barely audible.

"Let me see," she said as she approached him. Michael reluctantly showed his hand, marked with a small red spot where the hen had pecked him.

"It's okay—just a little peck," she said, rubbing his hand gently. "I bet it frightened you more than anything, right?"

Michael nodded, his lower lip trembling slightly.

"It's my fault, dear," Kathleen said, placing her hand gently on his back. "I made her angry, and she took it out on you."

Michael sniffled, his shoulders slumping with disappointment. "But I dropped the basket," he said, his voice wavering.

"I think I would have dropped the basket too if I got such a rude surprise," Kathleen chuckled.

John reached over and affectionately ruffled Michael's hair. "And you were very brave," he said warmly. "Not everyone can say they've faced down an angry hen."

Michael smiled at John's words, his confidence bolstered by his uncle's words.

"And you know what? We can still have a great time together," Kathleen continued. "Even if we hit a little bump in the road, how about we go brush the goats together? They've been waiting for us, and I think they'd love to see you."

But Michael didn't respond as Kathleen hoped. "I hate the country, and I hate farm animals," he declared, stomping his right foot on the barn floor.

Kathleen kept the conversation positive. "It takes some getting used to, but I'm sure you'll love getting to know our animals and helping look after them. Before long, you might even learn to ride Frisky."

While Michael smiled briefly at the mention of riding, Kathleen sensed it was time to change the subject.

"Now, I bet you'd like to water the garden. How about we unroll the longest garden hose you've ever seen, and you water the flower garden, then move on to the vegetables? Maybe we'll even pick some strawberries for dessert tonight."

Before she could finish, Michael stood up from the bale and dashed toward the barn door. "See if you can roll out the hose, honey. I'll catch up with you."

"Nice job, Mama," John said, gently touching her arm. "He's becoming quite the little man."

"Thanks, dear, that's kind of you to say. I just wish I'd been more patient—asking him to wait while I gathered the eggs under Red. I should have known that Red might react the way she did, and I should have made sure Michael wasn't in harm's way."

"Don't beat yourself up about it, Kathleen. We're all just learning."

"I know, hon. The good news is that his confidence will come through once he starts watering. He seems to trust me again, but time will tell."

As she headed toward the barn door, she glanced back at John with a sheepish grin. "I can see that being a mom isn't all that easy."

## 9

Kathleen glanced at the hose reel—130 feet of hose still wound neatly, just as John had left it. Her gaze swept the area, but Michael was nowhere in sight. *Had he gone inside? Maybe to use the bathroom or grab a drink of water?*

As she turned toward the kitchen, a flash of bright white caught her eye—a hen sauntering down the wood chip trail, away from the henhouse. Kathleen gasped. She hurried forward just in time to see five more hens slipping through the open door, making their escape.

She quickly shut the henhouse door and rushed toward the flock, hoping to get ahead of them and herd them back inside. What followed was a comical dance—her arms waving, feet shuffling—as she tried to corral the feathery escapees. But the hens had other ideas, darting in all directions, clucking and flapping their wings in chaotic glee. Michael was still nowhere in sight.

Kathleen darted back and forth, arms outstretched as she tried to steer the wayward hens toward the henhouse. A glance at the farm gate reassured her—it was closed. Breathing a sigh of relief, she turned back to the chaos, calling gently to the hens as she coaxed them forward. "Come on, chickens, back you go."

The hens, however, reveled in their newfound freedom, scattering in all directions as if playing a game of mischief. "Oh my gosh," Kathleen exclaimed, spotting John hurrying toward the chaos.

Undaunted, John and Kathleen fell into a familiar rhythm —farm life had prepared them for moments like this. Their laughter blended with the clucking cacophony as they worked together, determined to wrangle the hens back home.

Once the hens were safely back inside, Kathleen turned to John. "Have you seen Michael?"

John grinned. "No, but that's not surprising, is it?"

Kathleen sighed. He was more amused than she would have liked at the moment. "We might be in for a wild ride with this little scamp," she said.

"Right." Kathleen sighed. "You know, I bet he's used to getting into trouble for this kind of behaviour," she said thoughtfully. "We don't want to encourage it, but..." She hesitated. "We need to find a way to show him it's not okay while making sure he knows we still love him—no matter what. I don't know, John. This is all new territory for me."

After calling his name and scanning the area, Kathleen headed to the house while John searched farther afield.

Upstairs, she found Michael's bedroom door closed. Knocking lightly, she called his name in a friendly voice, determined to keep her tone warm despite the trouble he'd caused. When there was no response, she slowly pushed the door open.

Michael sat on the carpet, his back resting against the bed, Henley curled in his lap. He looked up at Kathleen but kept stroking the cat, his fingers moving in a steady rhythm. She stepped inside, crossing to the window, and pushing it open wide, letting in fresh air.

Kathleen called out to John, letting him know Michael was safe. Once he acknowledged her, she settled cross-legged on the floor beside Michael, who showed no hint of remorse.

"I understand why you're upset, sweetheart," she said gently. "But do you think letting the hens out was a good idea?"

Michael grinned. "They don't like living in a cage. I was just helping them out."

"A dog could attack them when they're running loose like that," Kathleen said gently. "They're not used to being outside their home, and they don't know the dangers. So, sweetheart, you weren't really helping them."

Michael shifted, gathering Henley into his arms and holding him close to his chest. Instead of responding, he changed the subject. "Listen to him purr, Auntie. He's a happy camper."

Kathleen smiled, sensing that the change of subject was a good opportunity to shift gears. She tousled Michael's hair, rising awkwardly from the floor. "Tomorrow is a whole new day, sweetheart. After breakfast, we can talk about all the things there are to explore on the farm and decide together where to start. Sound good, Michael?"

He raised an eyebrow, his gaze lingering on her for a moment as if unsure. "Uh-huh," he mumbled. "What's for lunch, Auntie?"

"That depends," Kathleen said with a playful grin. "Hamburgers or roast beef sandwiches? What'll it be?"*

"Can we have cheeseburgers and fries?" Michael's brown eyes twinkled as if he could already taste his favourite meal.

"Cheeseburgers, yes; fries, not today," Kathleen replied with a smile. "But if you like fries, wait 'til we hit the Shriners' food truck at the Saturday market. They've got the best fries around, no kidding."

Michael scrambled to his feet, gently plopping Henley onto

his bed. The cat stretched out and then settled into the covers, easily making himself at home in his next cozy spot.

"Oh, by the way, honey," Kathleen said, "did you brush your teeth this morning?"

Michael stared at the floor, shrugging his shoulders.

"Okay, let's do this together," Kathleen said, heading toward the ensuite bathroom. "After you, mister," she added, gesturing for Michael to go ahead of her.

After helping him step up onto the small wooden bench and brush his teeth thoroughly, Kathleen asked if she could take a look inside his mouth. When he opened wide, she knew she had made some progress. She held her breath against the foul odor, struggling to see in the dim bathroom light. She retrieved a flashlight from the vanity drawer and took a closer look.

"When's the last time you saw a dentist, dear?"

Michael shut his mouth, looking up at her. "I've never been to a dentist, Auntie."

Hiding her true emotions, Kathleen smiled softly. "I think you'd like Dr. Grant. She's great with kids, and she knows how to make your teeth and gums healthy again, sweetheart."

Michael furrowed his brow, intrigued. "What's it like, going to the dentist?"

Kathleen paused for a moment, then smiled sweetly, doing her best to ease his worries. "Dr. Grant will take a good look at your teeth and gums and figure out how to make them healthy again. She has an assistant who loves working with kids, too, and she'll be there to help. They even make it fun for kids so they enjoy their visit."

Michael's curiosity deepened. "What kind of fun things, Auntie?"

Kathleen chuckled softly. "Well, I've seen kids wearing funny glasses and watching cartoons while the dentist works on them. I'm not sure what they do at Dr. Grant's office, but I'm sure they'll have something fun for you, too."

Michael seemed satisfied with the explanation and hopped off the bench. "Can we have cheeseburgers now, Auntie?"

# 10

Shirley's visits to the farm became less frequent as Michael settled more comfortably into his new surroundings. With each passing day, he grew more curious about the world around him.

"What happened to those trees, Auntie?" Michael asked, his dark brown eyes filled with curiosity.

"Oh, my dear sweet Michael," Kathleen replied, gently running her hand over the brittle, copper-coloured bark. "Isn't that the most glorious colour? Arbutus trees are native to British Columbia. There's nothing wrong with them; it's just that the peeling bark is typical of arbutus trees. A lot of people think they're diseased, though," she chuckled. Kathleen often used bigger words when talking to Michael, thinking it might help expand his vocabulary.

Dabbing her brush in a pot of copper-colored paint, Kathleen continued working on her painting of the arbutus tree at her easel. Michael peeled some of the flaking bark from the tree, revealing the greenish wood underneath.

"They often grow along rocky bluffs, just like this one. And guess what? The native people of Vancouver Island used arbutus bark and leaves to make medicines for colds, stomach problems, and even tuberculosis."

"Hmm," Michael muttered, climbing onto a large outstretched limb almost touching the ground. "The leaves are crackly."

"They sure are," Kathleen agreed, her eyes bright with the joy of sharing this knowledge. "You can hear them rustle when the wind blows."

"What're we going to do today, Auntie?" Michael asked, eager to move on to the next adventure.

SCHOOL WAS SET to begin in September, and Kathleen and John had spent the spring and summer helping Michael adjust to his new surroundings. Their growing love for him deepened their understanding of parenthood, strengthening the emotional bond between the three of them.

One afternoon in August, Michael left the pen door open, letting the billy goat escape after John told him he couldn't have a second helping of ice cream. Kathleen and John had been working to reduce the sugar in Michael's diet to protect his newly restored dental work. Like any child, he became hyperactive after consuming too many sugary treats.

Kathleen's cousin Maggie, along with her children, Natalie and Robert, had taken the early morning ferry from Victoria to visit and spend some time on the farm. Even though Michael was eight, the age difference didn't seem to matter as they raced across the expansive lawns and explored the animal enclosures. Robert, six and named after his great-grandfather, and four-year-old Natalie brought a lively energy to the place. Kathleen missed living closer to her niece and nephew, having formed strong bonds with them when she lived nearby.

Kathleen cautioned Maggie, "We'll need to keep a close eye

on them, so they don't wander near the milldam. I told Michael to stay away from there while his cousins are here." She knew better than to rely on an eight-year-old to supervise the younger two.

Michael tried to shift the blame onto his cousin Robert, claiming he wouldn't have known the goat would head straight for the vegetable garden and devour the fresh lettuces, turnip greens, and strung-up broad beans flourishing there. But Kathleen and John both knew that Maggie and the kids had left right after lunch. If the door to the billy goat's pen had been left ajar, the feisty goat would have made its escape then.

John hammered a nail into a loosened board around the sheep pasture when he thought he heard the bleat of a goat—but not from the direction of the pen.

Investigating, John didn't need to look long before spotting the marauding, hairy white billy goat, greedily devouring plants and tearing through the once orderly vegetable garden. Lettuce and turnip greens were uprooted, soil scattered in their wake.

Horrified, he sprinted toward the garden, praying he wasn't too late to save what was left of the vegetables. The goat trampled over carrots, radishes, and peppers, grazing without a care. It reared up when it spotted John charging toward it, legs kicking high and head lowered, its sharp horns glinting. John knew he didn't have a chance against an aggressive goat, so he veered off course toward the barn.

Inside, he grabbed a thick rope, quickly fashioning a lasso with steady hands, hoping his skills hadn't dulled. Moving cautiously, he started back toward the garden, taking a wide detour to approach the goat from behind.

The sweet, pulpy scent of pumpkin distracted the goat just long enough for John to slip the lasso over its head. He tightened it quickly, securing the stubborn creature despite its defiance. With the mess of pumpkin guts smeared across its face and hooves, John dragged the goat back to its pen.

In the kitchen, he reported the devastating news to Kathleen.

"He destroyed the whole garden," he said, his voice heavy with frustration.

Kathleen's eyes widened in shock, disbelief momentarily freezing her in place. Then, as the news sank in, she let out a deep sigh, shaking her head in frustration.

"I told Michael not to go near the billy goat," she said, her voice tight. "He knows better. A strong kick from that goat could kill a child."

After listening to Michael's explanation, Kathleen took him by the hand, and the three of them walked quietly to the garden. Before them lay a disheveled landscape of overturned earth and plant remnants.

"Do you have any idea, Michael, how much work goes into making a garden like this?" John didn't wait for an answer. "There's tilling, planting seed, weeding, watering, picking... all so we can have fresh vegetables on our table."

Michael squirmed, trying to loosen Kathleen's grip on his hand.

"What do you have to say for yourself, Michael?" asked Kathleen, her patience slipping. "This is just too much."

Michael stayed silent, no longer attempting to blame anyone else for his mistake.

Perhaps sensing that Kathleen had reached her limit, John intervened.

"How can you make this up to us, Michael? How are you going to make this better, huh?" His voice was controlled, but tight with restrained temper as he pressed for accountability.

"I, um... well."

*At least he's giving it some thought*, Kathleen reassured herself. In those early months at Cliffhouse, he hadn't shown much remorse for his mischief, but she could see that was changing. Still, he needed to face the consequences of his actions. She was ready to step in if needed, but she hoped he'd take responsibility on his own. With Grade 3 just around the corner, this felt like an important moment for him. So she waited, giving him the space to respond.

Finally, in a hushed voice, he committed to gathering up all the leftover leaves and debris and placing them in the compost bin.

"Yes, and then what?" asked John sternly.

"Then, I guess I could get a hoe or a rake or something and smooth the earth so it doesn't look so ugly."

"That's a solid plan, Michael," John said, softening slightly. "And since it's cooling down now, you can start that right away."

After Michael began clearing the debris, Kathleen and John sat on the veranda, conversing softly while keeping a watchful eye on him.

"I feel good about how that went. What about you, honey?" Kathleen asked John.

"Yeah, it turned out well, but I'm still pretty upset about the damage. Aren't you?"

"I am, John. But we can't do anything about that now. Hopefully, he learned a valuable lesson today. I have to tell you, though, I worry about how easily he lies."

## 11

Kathleen smiled warmly at Michael. "How about we visit the schoolyard today so you can see where you'll be starting Grade 3 next week?"

Michael shook his head, his face scrunching up. "I don't want to go to school, Auntie. I just want to stay here with you and Uncle John."

Kathleen chuckled softly. "I know, sweetheart. But everyone goes to school. You'll probably see Ricky there, and you'll make some new friends too. I'm excited for you to start at Chickadee Elementary."

Michael's frown deepened, but he didn't argue further.

Kathleen's friend Marsha and her husband Tom had a son the same age as Michael. She invited Marsha and Ricky to visit them at the farm at the end of July and again two weeks later, in mid-August.

During their visits, Michael eagerly showed Ricky his favourite spots around the farm. Together, they explored the henhouse, the goat pen, and the milldam.

One day, Michael led Ricky to his secret hideaway in the

hayloft. Ascending the ladder, Michael turned to his friend with excitement and said, "Not even my aunt and uncle know about this place."

Ricky, whose parents owned the bustling garden centre in Ganges, was intrigued by farm life. Marsha's eyes sparkled with delight as she took in the abundance of fruit, vegetables, and blooming flowers at Cliffhouse Farm.

At the Open House at Chickadee Elementary in late August, Kathleen approached the Grade Three teacher, Mrs. Kennedy. After introducing herself and Michael, Kathleen suggested that Michael go outside to the playground, allowing her and Mrs. Kennedy a chance to talk. Michael eagerly agreed, happy to revisit the playground where Kathleen had brought him several times over the summer.

Kathleen leaned in slightly, her voice soft. "I thought you might want to know a bit about Michael's background," she began. She shared with Mrs. Kennedy that Shirley had been battling cancer and that Michael had been living apart from his mother since April. She also mentioned that his father had passed away.

Mrs. Kennedy's forehead furrowed with concern. "Oh, dear. Such a traumatic experience for a young child. How is he coping, Kathleen?"

"It's been a big adjustment for him, certainly," Kathleen acknowledged, "but overall he's been doing remarkably well. My husband John and I have grown very close to Michael during this time. Still, I must admit, I'm a bit nervous about him starting a new school." Kathleen confessed.

"Don't worry," Mrs. Kennedy said warmly. "We'll take good care of him here at Chickadee. It's a tight-knit community on this island, as you know. Children tend to form strong friendships and look forward to coming to school."

As Kathleen listened to Mrs. Kennedy's reassuring words,

she felt a sense of relief. "Thank you, Mrs. Kennedy. I appreciate your kindness and understanding. I'm sure Michael will thrive here."

**12**

September fifth arrived swiftly. Kathleen helped Michael choose his outfit for the first day of school, carefully draping the pieces over his desk chair. She pointed out that his wide-legged black jeans would go with any top and suggested a red, white, and black striped turtleneck pullover. To complete the look, she retrieved a wide black belt from his highboy dresser.

"Adios, Michael," John said, wrapping him in a warm hug. "Can't wait to hear all about your day when you get home. See you soon."

As they stepped into the front hall, Kathleen took Michael's denim jacket from the coat hook. "It's chilly this morning, honey. You might need this."

Michael adored his new fleece-lined jacket—it was just like John's. As he slipped it on, Kathleen noticed a subtle shift in his demeanor. He seemed quieter than usual, but of course, he was starting school.

Michael grabbed his backpack, and they headed down the driveway in Kathleen's cream-colored Oldsmobile Cutlass.

At the school, they were met with the lively hum of children's laughter and the energetic buzz of the schoolyard. Kathleen scanned the playground, hoping to spot Ricky. Nearby, a cluster of backpacks rested on the ground near the front entrance. Michael set his down, then stood still, his expression unreadable as he took in the playground full of unfamiliar faces. Kathleen understood—without the advantage of starting at Chickadee in kindergarten, he would feel like the outsider he was.

Soon, she spotted Ricky hurrying toward them. Kathleen gave Michael a quick hug, greeted Ricky, and turned to leave. "Okay, bye, honey. I'll pick you up at 2:15. If you're not in the playground, I'll look for you in the school."

Michael skipped off with Ricky without looking back.

ON THE DRIVE HOME, Kathleen's emotions swirled. She was happy Michael was starting school on Sunrise Island but tearful at the thought of him no longer being home all day. She had grown so used to his constant presence—the joys, the challenges, all of it—and she adored her little sidekick to pieces.

Back in her kitchen, she felt unmoored, unsure of what to do with herself despite the endless demands of farm life. The house felt oddly quiet, an undeniable void settling in.

Wandering outside, she found John tending to the vegetable garden. "Gosh, I sure didn't think I'd feel this sad about Michael starting school," she admitted.

John chuckled. "Yeah, I thought you'd be swinging from the rafters."

Kathleen laughed at the joke. "It's silly, I know. But I'll take my cue from you, my love, and keep busy. Five hours will fly by."

"Indeed," John said, raising an eyebrow. "It'll be a long day for him. Who knows what kind of mood he'll be in when he gets home."

"I know," Kathleen sighed. "Let's hope it's a good one. At least he had Ricky with him—so far, so good."

John grinned. "Maybe a bowl of his favourite chocolate pudding would help."

Kathleen chuckled. "I know, John. I know."

# 13

Kathleen pulled into the school parking lot at 2:00, determined not to look too eager. She busied herself flipping through the latest issue of *People,* but couldn't focus on it.

The moment she spotted Michael, she clenched her teeth. His shoulders were slumped, his steps slow and heavy. Something was wrong.

She stepped out of the car and waved so he'd see her.

As soon as he slid into the front seat, she turned to him. "What happened, honey?"

"Just drive, Auntie. Please."

She hesitated but put the car in gear. "I'm sorry you had a rough day," she said gently. Then she frowned. "Oh—where's your jacket?"

Michael's jaw tensed. "Mom," he growled, "just go."

Kathleen's grip tightened on the wheel. Once they were on the road, she tried again. "Did you leave it on the playground?"

Michael kicked hard under the dashboard. "No. They took it." His voice wavered, and she saw him fighting to hold back tears.

Kathleen pulled over, her pulse quickening. She rested a gentle hand on Michael's shoulder. "Who took it, sweetheart?"

"I don't know their names," he muttered. "The same kids who laughed at my name. They called me Mickey."

Kathleen's heart sank. *His first day, and already he's been singled out.* She wasn't sure whether to comfort him, march back to the school, or distract him with something sweet.

She made her decision. Ignoring his protests, she drove to the corner store and bought him a butterscotch ice cream cone. "Here, honey," she said, offering it to him. "You eat this while I take care of things."

Alone in the locked car, Michael licked his cone as Kathleen strode toward the school.

"MR. FISHER, I have to say, I didn't expect bullying to be an issue at a school like Chickadee." Kathleen's voice was calm, but there was no mistaking the disappointment beneath it.

"After she let him know what had happened, the vice-principal shook his head, his brows furrowed in disbelief. "I'm shocked to hear this," he said, his voice steady but filled with concern. 'Trust me, it's not the norm here."

Kathleen wasn't convinced.

"I'll look into it right away," he promised. "And if necessary, we'll involve the police."

BY THE NEXT DAY, it was clear the incident hadn't involved Chickadee students. Mr. Fisher confirmed as much when he called Kathleen with an update.

"Turns out, this was the work of a couple of bad apples from the neighbourhood," he said.

Kathleen's grip on the phone tightened. "How did outsiders get onto the school grounds?"

"We have staff supervising during recess, but they didn't notice anything unusual," he admitted. "Our security cameras, however, tell a different story."

She listened intently as he explained.

"The two boys slipped in through the front gate while classes were in session. When students came out for recess, they blended in. Michael was in the wrong place at the wrong time."

"How old were they?"

"Older. Around twelve."

Kathleen exhaled sharply. "Typical bully tactic—picking on kids who can't fight back."

"That's right," Mr. Fisher agreed. "I'm sorry this happened, especially on Michael's first day." He opened a closet and pulled out a familiar jacket. "It's a bit dirty but otherwise intact."

"Oh, thank goodness." Kathleen's breath caught as she almost said *my son*—but stopped herself. "Michael will be relieved."

"The police acted quickly," Mr. Fisher continued. "After they put out an alert, someone at the Sunrise Café spotted one of the boys wearing a jacket matching the description. That tip led them straight to the culprits."

"That was fast," Kathleen said, impressed. "I can't thank you enough."

"It was a team effort," he said, his voice carrying quiet satisfaction. "The boys will be doing community service for the next few months. They're on our radar now. I don't think this will happen again."

～

Back in the car, Kathleen watched Michael's face light up as she handed him the jacket.

"Did they get in trouble?" he asked eagerly.

"You bet they did," she said. "Now, tomorrow is a new day. Don't give those boys another thought. You're safe at Chickadee, and you're safe at the farm." She ruffled his hair. "Now, how about a cheeseburger?"

Michael's eyes widened. "With fries?"

"How about fries *and* a shake?" Kathleen grinned. "I feel like I could eat a horse. We'll bring some home for Uncle John, too."

# 14

As the school year unfolded, Michael settled in. His confidence grew, friendships formed, and before long, he was the boy everyone wanted to visit—because, really, who wouldn't want to see the farm where Michael lived? With each passing day, he found his place in this new world, a world that, just a short while ago, had felt so foreign.

Days turned into weeks and weeks into months as Michael embraced the rhythms of small-town life. Amidst the ever-changing seasons and the steady pulse of farm chores and school days, he found a deep sense of belonging. Kathleen and John, once just his aunt and uncle, had become his steadfast guides, offering unwavering support through the challenges of growing up.

As time stretched on, Michael's connection with them deepened. Their bond, forged through shared laughter, tears, and moments of quiet understanding, grew stronger with each passing day. Though the duration of his stay remained uncertain, one thing was clear—Cliffhouse Farm had become more than just a place to live. To Michael, it was his sanctuary, his haven, his second home.

Michael made new friends, and Kathleen socialized with their parents, helping Michael integrate into the community. Every Saturday afternoon, on the softball diamond, she and John proudly cheered him on as he played for the "Sunrise Warriors."

That evening, after Michael went to bed, Kathleen and John enjoyed a quiet liqueur on the veranda, reflecting on their experience of parenting.

"Listen, honey," John began, "it's simple. Kids will stumble, they'll err, and they'll sometimes make choices we don't agree with. Our job as parents is to guide them, establish boundaries, and hold them accountable when they veer off course."

"Absolutely," Kathleen nodded. "We're not exempt from making mistakes ourselves. Parenting is a journey filled with ups and downs." Kathleen's tone softened. "Michael can test our patience at times, but we'll keep doing our best. He needs to know that we're here for him, no matter what."

## 15

The last day of school held the promise of joy, but in the Mitchell household and throughout the tight-knit community of Sunrise Island, it felt as though the sun would never rise again.

Kathleen was restless, tossing and turning in bed, leaving John without covers. He awoke groggily, his voice thick with sleep. "What's wrong, love? Is it Michael's leaving?"

Nuzzling her face into John's sturdy shoulder, Kathleen let out a sob. "I can't bear to see our boy go," she lamented. Yet she knew she was being unreasonable. Shirley was healthy again—at least for the time being—and her prognosis was promising. They had declared her cured, with minimal chance of recurrence for at least fifteen years.

John continued to stroke Kathleen's back, offering comfort through his touch. "I understand, love. It's a lot for him to handle at his age," he murmured. "But we'll make sure he knows we're here for him, no matter what. We're only a 35-minute ferry ride away."

John paused, his gaze gentle as he met Kathleen's eyes. "We'll stay connected, no matter where he is."

"I know," Kathleen persisted, her voice thick with emotion. "But the poor little guy is only nine, and now he faces another major shift. He's made friends here, and he likes his school. I wish he could stay." Kathleen released herself from John and rolled over to grab a tissue from the bedside table.

"Kids are resilient, honey," John reassured her. "Don't worry about Michael. He and Shirley can visit us as often as they want."

After blowing her nose, Kathleen brightened a little. "Yes, that's true, John," she said, propping herself up with her pillow. "And he'll have a whole different set of friends here." She smiled inwardly, trying to reassure herself—*maybe it's not so bad after all.*

But then the doubt crept back in.

"You know, John," Kathleen said softly, "caring for Michael for over a year now has taught me what motherhood is all about."

John, now fully awake, shifted to a sitting position and placed his hand over hers. He listened intently, nodding in agreement as Kathleen spoke.

"I have a deeper understanding of the responsibilities and joys of motherhood now," she said with a firm resolve.

Smiling, John urged her to continue.

"And I know that motherhood isn't solely defined by genetics. I've learned that motherhood is about more than biological ties—it's about love, sacrifice, and nurturing," she said thoughtfully.

"You're absolutely right, Kathleen," John replied, his voice warm and full of admiration. "You've been an incredible mother figure to Michael, and I have no doubt that your love and guidance have made a lasting impact on him."

"*Our* love and guidance, dear," Kathleen corrected softly. She leaned over and kissed John briefly on the lips before continuing. "And, John," she added quietly, "let's keep trying."

John's smile grew as he listened to Kathleen, his eyes tender. "I get it, Kathleen, and I'm right there with you. Whether it's through adoption or conception, I'm committed to building our family together, however it may come to be."

He leaned in to kiss her forehead. "Our journey to parenthood may be unconventional, but as long as we're together, I know we'll find our way."

After a brief pause, John continued with a twinkle in his eye. "And if parenting Michael has reignited your desire to have a baby, then I'm all in."

**16**

———

It had all been arranged, discussed, and agreed upon. Shirley would pick up Michael and his belongings the day after school let out for the summer.

Kathleen rose early on the last day of school, determined to make it special for Michael. She carefully prepared his lunch, adding his favorite peanut butter and jelly sandwich along with watermelon, carrot sticks, and Smarties. As a final touch, she taped a congratulatory note to the inside of his lunchbox, making sure he wouldn't miss it.

*Michael,*

*We're so proud of you!*
*We love you forever.*
*Have an awesome day, buddy!*

*Auntie Kathleen and Uncle John*
*XOXO*

**17**

———————

Michael bounced down the stairs and made a beeline for the kitchen. "Auntie, did you remember my Smarties?" he asked eagerly.

"You bet, buddy. A special treat for my special guy," Kathleen replied with a smile.

As Michael gulped down a glass of milk and drowned his French toast with maple syrup, John called from the front hall. "Kathleen, can you come here for a moment?"

In the hallway, John asked, "What time will Shirley be here tomorrow, love?"

"She'll take the early ferry and be here for breakfast, just like I asked. I plan to make Michael's favourite apple pancakes for his farewell breakfast." Kathleen's voice held a hint of sadness.

When she returned to the kitchen, Michael had disappeared. Hmm, not like him to leave any of his French toast behind.

Kathleen stuffed his lunchbox into his backpack and called up the stairs, "Time to get going, sweetheart. The train's leaving!" She said it with a teasing tone, one she often used when Michael lagged.

DELIVERING Michael to Chickadee Elementary for the last time, Kathleen was torn between joy and sadness. He'd graduated to grade four after a year that had left him feeling accepted and encouraged. But she had gotten used to driving him to and from school, softball, and all around the island. She knew she would miss those moments, the ones she had come to cherish. *Stop feeling sorry for yourself*, she chided inwardly.

"I'll pick you up at 2:15, darling," she said as Michael exited the car, barely pausing to offer a goodbye.

*He's probably sad to be leaving the school and all his friends here,* she thought. *Why wouldn't he be?*

BACK IN MICHAEL'S ROOM, Kathleen began packing his belongings for the trip back to Victoria. Inside the box that Shirley had originally packed, she placed a surprise gift—a model of the Apollo Moon Rocket with engine sounds, flashing lights, and separation. Kathleen's only regret was that she wouldn't be there to see his face when he opened it.

She was lost in thought, imagining Michael's reaction to the gift, when John's voice broke through, startling her. He appeared in the doorway, leaning against the frame with his arms crossed over his broad chest.

"Michael will settle back home in no time, sweetheart," John said, his voice steady. "Once he reconnects with his old friends and gets back to his school, things will feel normal again."

"Yes," Kathleen replied, finding reassurance in his words. "And he and Shirley can visit us whenever they want."

"I'm guessing that might be sooner than we think," John added with a chuckle.

"Why? What do you mean, honey?"

"I overheard Michael talking to Shirley on the phone a few nights ago. He told her he didn't want to leave here."

Kathleen's heart warmed at the thought, but a pang of sadness for Shirley followed quickly. "Oh…"

"Yes," John continued. "And Shirley said he asked her if they could come and live with us."

Kathleen crossed the room and gently placed her hands on John's face, her voice thick with emotion. "We ought to be proud, John. I think we did a good job, don't you?"

"We did a stellar job, my love," he replied, kissing her softly. "Now, I have two questions: What time are we leaving to collect our sweet boy today? And do you want me to carry that box downstairs?"

"Two o'clock sharp, John," she chuckled. "The treasure box is packed and ready to go."

## 18

Kathleen had planned a special day to celebrate Michael's graduation—ice cream sundaes, shopping for a new skateboard at Carrington's, and a surprise dinner with Ricky and his parents. But today, instead of the usual excitement on the last day of school, the air felt strangely still. The schoolyard, typically alive with laughter and chatter, seemed eerily quiet.

"This doesn't feel right," John muttered, his gaze sweeping over the silent yard.

Kathleen's stomach fluttered as anxiety began to gnaw at her. She scanned the familiar faces, searching for Michael, her heart racing with an unsettling sense of dread. She could feel the panic creeping up as she approached one of Michael's teachers.

"Hi, Cathy. Have you seen Michael?" she asked, her voice a bit higher than usual.

Cathy's expression faltered. She exchanged a glance with John before motioning for them to follow her into the school. Inside, Cathy spoke briefly to the secretary and asked her to let Principal Marion Riley know they'd arrived.

The principal invited them into her office, but her flushed face and furrowed brow did little to ease their worry. "Michael's not here," she began, but Kathleen interrupted, her voice rising in disbelief.

"What do you mean, he's not here?" Kathleen exclaimed, struggling to process the words.

"Please, have a seat," Marion said, gesturing toward the two chairs in front of her large oak desk.

Kathleen, her nerves on edge, hardly felt like sitting. She perched on the edge of the visitor's chair, leaning forward as though that might somehow bring her closer to the truth. In a measured voice, she asked, "Where is Michael, Marion?"

Marion hesitated for a moment before speaking, each word deliberate. "He was last seen outside during lunch, playing in the cedar grove—it's a spot the kids like. I spoke with Eddie McLaughlin, the playground supervisor. He said the kids were weaving in and out of the trees, and he didn't notice Michael with anyone in particular. The playground was packed, especially on the last day of school, and it's hard for one person to keep track of every student."

Kathleen's anxiety spiked. "So, Michael's missing?"

John's voice was sharp with concern as he echoed his wife's words. "Our Michael is missing?"

"I know this is difficult," Principal Riley said softly, her eyes full of sympathy. "But we're doing everything we can."

John turned to her, his voice tight with concern. "Did you call his mother?"

"Yes," Marion replied. "She's on her way. She said she'll be on the next ferry."

"Is anyone else missing?" Kathleen held her breath, waiting for a response.

"Yes," Marion answered. "Tommy Vale. We called his parents as soon as we confirmed his absence, and they were just as concerned. We couldn't get through to you, Kathleen—were you at home?"

Kathleen's mind raced. She'd been busy with the preparations for dinner and had missed the call.

"We've contacted the RCMP," Marion continued. "A search is already underway."

KATHLEEN SAT MOTIONLESS, the gravity of the situation slowly settling in, while John rose from his chair, his body taut and alert. She absorbed Marion's words, but her mind was still clouded with disbelief. "Are they searching for Michael?" she asked, her voice trembling as tension coiled through her. The flashing lights of a migraine flashed in her vision, underscoring the impact of what had happened.

"You'll need to file a 'Missing Persons Report' at the station, but yes, the police are aware Michael is missing. It's just the paperwork that needs to be done first," Marion explained, her tone gentle but firm.

Kathleen didn't hesitate. She reached for the phone on Marion's desk, dialing the local RCMP office without a second thought. After 22 years of knowing Officer Bill, she hoped he could offer some sign of progress.

While Kathleen made her call, John spoke calmly, his eyes fixed on Marion. "Did anyone search the area right outside the school grounds?"

Kathleen's heart pounded in her chest as she struggled to keep her panic in check. She had to remain calm, to think clearly. Deep down, she believed Michael wouldn't stray far from the school alone.

Marion answered, her voice steady but with a note of concern. "Yes, the police have organized a search team, including a tracking dog. There are fifty trained rescuers on the ground and volunteers from the community searching every-where—woods, lakes, all around the area."

Kathleen barely registered the rest of the conversation. When the receptionist at the police station finally picked up, she learned that Bill had joined the search team and that there were no updates yet. The words seemed to blur together as she slowly placed the receiver back in its cradle, a sense of helpless-ness settling in.

Marion, now standing, walked over to Kathleen and gently touched her shoulder. "Look, Kathleen, I know this must be a shock, but the boys have only been missing for an hour and a half. We need to be patient."

Kathleen fought the urge to lash out. *Don't patronize me, Marion.* She wanted to scream it, but instead, she clenched her fists and bit back the words. The first hour was critical in any missing person's case; Kathleen was well aware of that.

Gripped by panic, she stood abruptly and grabbed John's arm. He hesitated for a second, his face reflecting a mix of confusion and concern, but then he followed her as they rushed out of the office, down the hall, and into the parking lot.

John's voice broke through the panic. "Who is this Tommy kid? Do you know him, Kathleen?"

"Tommy's in grade five. He's not one of Michael's friends, as far as I know," Kathleen replied, furrowing her brow.

"Do you think that Michael ran away, Kathleen?" John asked, worry etched in his expression.

Kathleen paused, the idea hanging in the air between them. "Ran away?" she echoed, then shook her head. "Why would he..." Deep in thought, her words trailed off. "Do you think he overheard us talking this morning?" she asked after a moment.

She remembered the scene: Michael had left his breakfast half-eaten and disappeared upstairs. The realization struck her all at once.

John's expression tightened. "Maybe he overheard something—his emotional distress over leaving us, leaving his friends, this new school... It could have all been too much for him."

Kathleen nodded slowly, her heart heavy with the possibility. "Of course. He's only nine, John. Maybe he thought running away would solve everything—escape the pain of saying goodbye."

John looked away, his mind racing. "And Tommy... maybe he was someone Michael looked up to. Maybe he convinced him that if he ran away, he wouldn't have to go back to Victoria."

Kathleen let out a deep sigh as remorse settled in. *Had their words, their discussions of Michael's departure, triggered this?* "I never imagined our words might have made him feel rejected, but it's possible."

"He knew this day would come, Kath, but it's still a lot for a kid to handle."

"I think he was just overwhelmed, John. He didn't know how to manage all these big feelings."

John placed a hand on her arm. "Listen, we need to go home. We should be there in case the phone rings. Or, I could go searching while you stay. Just tell me what you want to do."

"Let's go home, dear. We need to be together. They're doing everything they can to find the boys. The last thing they need is panic."

"We need to be by the phone, too, in case Shirley calls," John said, his voice low. "She'll need us now more than ever."

TURNING INTO THEIR DRIVEWAY, John and Kathleen noticed Shirley's car parked in the turnaround. The sight of Shirley sitting on the veranda steps brought a ripple of tension through the air. Her figure appeared small against the vast expanse of the farmhouse.

As they got closer, Shirley stood, her eyes fixed on their approaching car. Without waiting for them to step out, she rushed toward Kathleen's Cutlass, her pace quickening with each step. She began pacing anxiously, her movements growing more restless as they finally opened the car doors.

"Tears welled in Shirley's eyes, her voice shaky as she tried to speak, her emotions overwhelming her. When John pulled her into an embrace, she broke down, a flood of tears spilling over. He held her tightly, offering what comfort he could as the sobs slowly subsided.

Kathleen, fighting her own emotions, gently placed a hand on Shirley's head. "We'll cry it out together, honey. Don't hold back."

INSIDE, the dining room was set up for a celebration that now seemed uncertain. The table was beautifully arranged, but no one had an appetite. Kathleen suggested a warm bath might help Shirley relax, but Shirley insisted on staying by the phone in the living room.

The house felt suffocatingly quiet that evening. Normally, Michael would run around, chasing Henley, cranking the TV volume up too loud, and rummaging through the pantry for snacks. Tomorrow, there will be no softball practice with John. No bath before bed, no bedtime story, no goodnight kiss.

As minutes dragged into agonizing hours, Kathleen's mind swirled with a mixture of emotions—fear, confusion, and a deep sense of helplessness. The absence of Michael on this pivotal day felt like a nightmare she couldn't wake from.

*What is happening right now? Is he safe? Is he hurt? Is he scared? Trying to reach us?*

The questions gnawed at her, unanswered and relentless. The worry in Kathleen's expression mirrored Shirley's, both women overwhelmed by the uncertainty surrounding Michael's whereabouts and well-being.

John and Kathleen agreed that there was nothing they could have done differently to prevent Michael's disappearance. Kathleen tried to reassure herself that it was true, but deep down, in the darkest corners of her mind, she couldn't shake the feeling of guilt.

**19**

———————

Michael's disappearance created an emptiness that words couldn't capture. Grief consumed them, their thoughts locked on the search for him. Kathleen and John worked together, compiling a list of anyone who might have a lead on Michael's whereabouts—friends, acquaintances, anyone who could offer a clue. They also noted places they frequented as a family, including their regular trips to Victoria. The news sent shockwaves through Maggie's and John's families. Everyone understood that the nightmare of a missing child was every parent's deepest fear.

Then came the call.

"Kathleen, we've found Michael." Bill's familiar voice on the other end of the line brought an overwhelming rush of relief to Kathleen. She quickly covered the mouthpiece and called out, "John! Shirley! They've found him!"

**20**

———————

Bill opened the door of his police car for Michael, and as the young boy stepped out, his eyes immediately locked on his mother's. "Mama," Michael cried out as he rushed toward her. Shirley's heart flooded with joy as she swept him up into her arms, offering the comfort they both had longed for.

Michael's eyes shimmered with tears as he nestled his head against her shoulder. They held each other tightly, savouring the moment of reunion. Shirley whispered words of reassurance and love, months of separation melting away.

Later, Shirley confided in Kathleen that Michael hadn't called her "Mama" since he was five years old.

Kathleen and John stepped back, giving them space, their hearts swelling with joy at the sight of mother and son reunited. Smiles and teary eyes reflected their shared happiness in the quiet of the moment. Watching them, Kathleen felt a quiet sense of connection with John, a reminder of the enduring strength of love and family.

Once the excitement of the reunion began to settle, the group gathered around the table, set for dinner.

Kathleen grinned, her voice light, "You see? I left this all set for a reason."

Shirley returned the smile warmly. "Let's save the heavy talk for after dinner. We could all use a break from the drama, at least for a while. And, honestly, I'm absolutely starving!"

Her smile was contagious, and a wave of lighthearted laughter filled the room, easing the day's tension.

AFTER DINNER, they carried warm drinks onto the veranda and settled into the evening air, the tranquil surroundings offering a fitting backdrop to discuss the trauma of Michael's disappearance. The quiet of the moment seemed almost surreal, as if the peace of the evening was in stark contrast to the whirlwind of emotions they'd all been through.

Kathleen and John had guessed correctly for the most part.

"No, Tommy's not one of my friends," Michael began, his cheeks flushing slightly. He hesitated, glancing down at his hands before meeting Shirley's gaze. It was clear he was struggling to find the right words.

"Tommy saw me crying in the school bathroom," Michael admitted, his voice wavering with emotion.

"It's okay, sweetheart. Please, go on," Kathleen encouraged softly. "We just want to understand what happened so we can help."

Shirley reached over and briefly touched Michael's shoulder in a gesture of reassurance. "We all love you so much," she said, her voice full of warmth. "We're just so glad you're home safe. Don't worry about anything; we need to know what happened, that's all."

John spoke up gently, trying to ease the tension. "What did Tommy say after you told him you didn't want to go back to Victoria... or at least, that's what I think you said," he added, trying to make it easier for Michael to open up in front of his mother.

Encouraged by their support, Michael's voice grew steadier. "Yeah, that's what I told him," he confirmed. "And he said I didn't have to go back. He said if I wanted, he could show me where to hide so no one would find us."

Kathleen noticed that Shirley seemed deep in thought. She imagined she was navigating the delicate balance between reprimanding her son for his impulsive behavior and encouraging him to open up more.

But Michael's wide eyes and earnest words were a poignant reminder of his innocence—just a nine-year-old boy who hadn't fully grasped the consequences of his actions.

Shirley's expression softened, and she met his gaze gently. "I understand, sweetheart," she said. "I can see how you might have thought that was the easy way out... without thinking it through, right?"

Michael nodded, his expression serious. "I just followed Tommy," he said, his voice quiet but sure. "He said he'd done it before, and it worked."

Kathleen's voice was tender as she spoke. "I'm guessing you left during lunch, right, darling?"

Michael nodded. "Yes, Mama," he replied. "We waited until the playground supervisor wasn't looking and hid behind the trees until everyone else went inside. Then we just opened the front gate and left."

As he relived the moment of escape, Michael smiled faintly. It was clear he felt a sense of triumph, unaware of the bigger picture. Little did they know that their escape had been captured on the school's security cameras.

John helped steer the conversation. "Where did you go?" he asked, his eyes focused on Michael.

"Um, well, I'm not sure. I just followed Tommy," Michael replied, taking a sip of his hot chocolate before continuing. The adults exchanged knowing glances, recognizing the innocence behind Michael's actions.

"I understand that you thought Tommy, being older, knew how to help you," Shirley said gently, her voice filled with empathy.

"Yes, Mama, I thought he could help me—at first. And then, I got worried," Michael admitted, his voice revealing his vulnerability.

"Worried?" Shirley prompted softly, her tone encouraging as she leaned in, hoping to coax the full story from her son.

Michael shifted uncomfortably in his chair, taking another sip of his drink before continuing, his embarrassment clear.

"Well...it all seemed okay for a while. I recognized some of the places we passed on our way into Ganges," Michael said, his voice hesitant. He paused, frowning. "But when Tommy led me into the marina, I didn't see a place to hide."

The adults nodded encouragingly, their eyes focused on Michael.

"We raced down the aisles between the boats, one after the other," Michael continued, his words tumbling out in a rush of adrenaline-fueled memories. "...until Tommy found what he was looking for. It was a fishing boat, Uncle John," he said, glancing at John as if seeking validation.

"Right," John replied with a smile, recalling the fishing trip they had taken last March. "What happened next, Michael?"

"Tommy went right over to the boat like it was his," Michael recounted, his eyes wide with the same amazement he'd felt at that moment. "He lifted the blue tarp and told me to get in the boat and under the tarp."

"That must've been difficult with the boat bobbing up and down in the water," Kathleen said, her analytical mind placing her right there on the dock.

It was, Auntie," Michael said with a nod. "But we made it.

Tommy pulled the tarp over us so no one would be able to find us, he said."

"What was it like under the tarp, honey?" Shirley asked, her voice gentle.

"Stinky and cold. And wet," Michael added, grimacing.

"I'm sure you remember it so clearly, sweetheart," Shirley said gently. "But talking about it will help, and in time, those memories won't feel so strong."

Michael smiled at his mother, seeming more at ease as he shared his story. He took another sip of hot chocolate before continuing. "We stayed quiet for a long time because Tommy said we didn't want anyone to hear us. But after a while, it got really hard to stay still, and my stomach started growling." He let out a small chuckle, drawing laughter from the others.

"Did you hear anyone calling for you, Michael?" John asked, wanting to hear the details firsthand, even though he, Kathleen, and Shirley had already heard the search-and-rescue account from Bill.

"Yes, but Tommy told me not to answer, so I didn't," Michael said. "I got really tired and stretched out as best I could on the floor of the boat."

Shirley nodded, her voice gentle with understanding. "I can only imagine how worn out you must've been—walking all that way from Chickadee to Ganges, worrying about running away, and then trying to sleep on those cold, wet boards with an empty stomach."

"Unfortunately," Michael continued, trying to stifle a giggle, "I kicked Tommy hard in the head while I was asleep, and he cried out. Next thing we knew, the tarp was pulled back, and a stranger called our names."

"What was that like, sweetheart?" Shirley asked. "Were you relieved that they found you?"

"Haha," Michael responded, now visibly more at ease. "Yes,

it felt good that they found us, but I was a little scared too," he admitted.

"That's understandable, Michael," John said gently. "You probably thought you were in big trouble, right?"

"Yeah, maybe, but not really. Most of all, I wanted a cheeseburger," he said with a grin. "And the people who found us were really nice. They laughed and cheered, so I wasn't worried about getting into trouble."

THE JOYOUS REUNION and heartfelt conversations brought the family even closer together. Now, the dreaded departure of Michael to rejoin his birth mother in Victoria seemed less daunting.

After loading Shirley's car with Michael's things, John and Kathleen prepared to say goodbye. Michael lifted Henley into his arms, hugged him tightly, and whispered, "Adios, Mr. Hen-Hen, I'll see you next week."

Watching Michael's cheerful demeanor and his apparent acceptance of the shift back to Victoria, Kathleen felt a surge of gratitude. She was happy for both Michael and Shirley, relieved that things had turned out the way they had.

"Yes," John said, pulling Michael into a hug. "Adios to you, my favourite nephew. Maybe when you come next weekend, we can start your riding lessons if you want."

Michael's face lit up at the thought of riding Frisky, a wide grin spreading across his face as he bounced in his seat.

As John walked to the driver's side to give Shirley a final hug, Kathleen wrapped Michael in a warm, extended embrace. "You're my favourite boy of all time, Michael; you know that, right?"

Michael smiled and whispered into her ear, "And you're my

favourite auntie of all time; you know that, right?" They both giggled, reluctant to let go, until Kathleen released him.

Kathleen and Shirley shared one last hug, their smiles brimming with affection for each other.

"Shirl, when you come this weekend, let's make a strawberry pie if you're up for it," Kathleen said, already looking forward to the harvest.

"Oh, I'm always up for a strawberry pie," Shirley replied, buckling her seatbelt. "But only if you've got some vanilla ice cream to go with it."

As Shirley's car tires crunched down the gravel driveway, both women waved heartily from their open windows, and Shirley gave the horn three quick blasts.

In the poignant moment, Kathleen and John, arms wrapped around each other's shoulders, stood there, feeling grateful, soaking in the happiness of the moment and the way everything had turned out.

**21**

———————

Kathleen and John slept soundly that first night, but as weeks and months passed, both began to struggle with insomnia. John, rising at 5:30 every morning, sometimes couldn't recall even falling asleep. Kathleen, too, found herself restless, her nights increasingly disturbed. Uncharacteristically, she started stocking bottles of red wine in the breakfront—a departure from her habit of keeping only a few bottles for guests or special occasions.

"Honey, since we both seem to have trouble sleeping, what do you think about taking an evening stroll together each night before bed?" John suggested.

"Sure, John. That sounds like a good idea," Kathleen replied.

"And I'm serious about it, sweetheart. Come rain, hail, wind, or snow, let's make a commitment and stick to it, okay?" John proposed earnestly.

Kathleen smiled, appreciating John's motivation—especially when he also suggested she try melatonin to help with her sleep. To bring some lightness to their evenings, they began watching comedy shows on television. Whenever John visited his old friend Stewart to commiserate over their shared cattle herd, Kathleen used the time to visit his wife, Amelia, at their farm.

Kathleen also began volunteering with the Lions Club, where she met Mary, a mother who had suffered the excruciating loss of her child. But unlike Kathleen's family, Mary's child had been abducted five years ago, with no clues to offer even a glimmer of hope.

As heartbroken as Kathleen was for Mary, hearing her story only deepened her gratitude for the happy ending their family had found.

## 22

————

A s the days and months blurred together with little change, John reached a conclusion he wanted to share with Kathleen. Earlier that day, while in the village, he found himself captivated by a tray of chocolate-covered strawberries displayed in the window of Sweetness Bakery. Inspired by the simple pleasure of seeing them, he bought half a dozen and added a cold bottle of bubbly from the liquor store's fridge.

On the veranda, John set up a romantic scene—he positioned a Parisian-style café table and chairs facing west, near the fragrant rose bushes. With a delicate pink tablecloth draped over the wrought-iron table, he arranged a sparkling crystal plate of strawberries and two chilled champagne glasses. It had been far too long since he and Kathleen had indulged in such pleasures.

Kathleen's eyes brightened at John's thoughtful gesture, recognizing the subtle message in his actions—to bring romance back into their lives. Surrounded by the golden light of the setting sun, she relaxed into the evening as John finally spoke.

"We have two choices, love. We can let this destroy us, or we can choose not to let it."

Kathleen absorbed his words, their quiet simplicity sinking in. She didn't want to dampen his spirit or dismiss the wisdom behind them, but her instinctive response came anyway.

"I just wish things could go back to the way they were, John. But I know they never will."

John gave a slow, thoughtful nod, his features softening.

"You're absolutely right, my love. Our lives are forever changed. But that doesn't mean we should let Michael's absence consume us. We must also cherish the good times. That boy continues to bring us so much joy. When we had the chance to care for him, we gave him stability and loved him as our own. My heart aches just as much as yours, but I think we have to acknowledge our humanity and accept that we've done everything within our power to have a child of our own. If it's meant to be, it will. We have no control over that."

**23**

———————

Farm life continued as it always had, with animals needing care and hayfields and lawns demanding attention. There were the spring and fall plantings, the harvesting, and the constant upkeep.

Kathleen and John both felt the absence of Michael keenly, but more pressing than that was the fact that they had not yet conceived a child of their own. They had heard stories of couples torn apart as they redirected their grief toward one another.

"Let's not let that happen to us, John," Kathleen said one evening at twilight as they walked to the barn to return their gardening tools.

Placing his Dutch hoe in the toolshed, John turned to her. "Babe, nothing—not even something as heart-wrenching as this—could tear apart what you and I share."

Kathleen's heart soared, buoyed by the deep sincerity in his words. She snuggled close, resting her head on his chest and feeling the comforting warmth of his soft flannel shirt against her cheek. He pulled her in tighter, and they held each other for a long moment in the quiet barn, the air thick with the scent of straw, while moonlight filtered through the gaps in the barn boards.

ON SUNDAY EVENING AT TWILIGHT, Kathleen wrapped herself in a red cashmere shawl and joined John on the veranda, where his legs were stretched out on the footrest of his favourite lounger. Before she could settle down, he excitedly gestured toward the distant maple grove. "Look at that, sweetheart. Our colder winter produced vibrant foliage—more like what we'd see back east."

Kathleen stepped up to the rail. "It's like an enormous bouquet from nature. I haven't seen such bright fall colours here in years," she said, admiring the sweeping reds, oranges, and yellows that painted the landscape like brushstrokes on a canvas.

"I know," John said. "You couldn't orchestrate that if you tried. It's like looking at a beautiful painting."

Kathleen sat beside him, letting the moment sink in. "How funny that we look at a real-life scene and compare it to a painting," she chuckled. "Shouldn't it be the other way around?"

"I don't know," John smiled, "that's far too analytical for me."

As the evening darkened and the temperature dropped, they were about to go inside when tiny flashes of light caught their attention. Looking toward the cornfield, they were reminded of Michael's wonder the first time he saw fireflies.

Savouring the moment, they stood quietly, wrapped in each other's arms. The bittersweet memory of the good times they'd shared with Michael tugged at Kathleen's heart. "That's Michael, popping in to say hello," she said fondly to John.

"Maybe it's a sign we'll have a child of our own someday, sweetheart."

"Let's go with that," Kathleen replied, smiling. "I'll believe it if you will."

She drew him closer. "Then let's believe it together, John. It's one reason I keep that ancient cradle in the attic—the one my mama rocked me in thirty-two years ago. It helps me hold onto hope that it'll come into use again one day."

John's voice softened. "Yes, I get it, sweetheart. We all find solace in different ways. But now..." He paused slightly, choosing his words carefully. "Since we have little control over these matters, why don't we focus on enjoying our lives here at Cliffhouse and nurturing the dreams we've shared for so long?"

Kathleen's face lit up with a radiant smile as she gazed at John. Rising on her tiptoes, she pressed her lips gently against his. As they embraced, they shared a deep, tender kiss, savouring the warmth and comfort of each other's presence under the cool night sky. Kathleen felt John's affection nourish her soul and spirit, a testament to their enduring love.

**24**

———

Kathleen was late. But that wasn't anything new. Her cycles, once as predictable as the turning of seasons, had become erratic since Michael no longer lived with them.

"I think there's something wrong, John." No 'Good morning,' no 'How did you sleep?' or 'It looks like a nice day.' Instead, Kathleen walked straight past John, who was frying eggs at the kitchen stove, heading toward the screen door.

John immediately turned off the stove and lifted the frying pan from the burner, setting it on an oven mitt on the counter. He walked over to Kathleen, gently placing his hands on her shoulders as she stood facing the outdoors. Pressing his cheek to hers, he asked softly, "What do you mean, my love?"

As Kathleen turned to face him, he took a step back, giving her space. "It's been three months now," she said despondently. "I've never been this late." She moved away and walked to the fridge, pulling out a bottle of orange juice. "I mean, maybe I'm entering early menopause or something. I don't know."

As she poured herself a glass, John gently urged her to visit Dr. Chalmers. "Please try not to worry about the unknown, sweetheart. If you make a doctor's appointment, I'd love to go with you, if that's okay. Maybe we can have lunch or go out to dinner afterward, depending on the timing."

Kathleen walked back to John, stood on her tiptoes, and kissed him gently on the lips before wrapping her arms around his neck. A smile spread across her face as she beamed, grateful as ever that she'd married the love of her life.

**25**

John and Kathleen sat comfortably in the examination room, anticipation fluttering in their hearts as they waited for Dr. Chalmers to return. When the door swung open, the doctor entered with a bright smile, skipping the formalities and diving straight into the news.

"Congratulations," she exclaimed, her grin infectious. "You're pregnant, Kathleen. Two months along."

Tears welled in both Kathleen's and John's eyes. Kathleen's shoulders trembled as she struggled to contain her emotions. "You're sure?" she asked, her voice wavering.

Dr. Chalmers and John shared a soft chuckle, the room brimming with joy. John's smile radiated happiness, and Kathleen's heart swelled with warmth.

"We'll truly have something big to celebrate this afternoon, doc. Thanks for the great news," John said, his voice thick with emotion.

"It's my pleasure, folks," Dr. Chalmers replied warmly. "Now, Kathleen, please see Breanne at the front desk to schedule your next appointments."

AT THE DRIFTWOOD Inn in Grace Square, they indulged in a feast of fresh seafood accompanied by a single glass of champagne. "I'll sip yours, dear. No alcohol for this precious baby of ours." Kathleen smiled, a joy John hadn't seen in two years.

"Do you know how sweet those words are, my love?" John asked, reaching across the table to take her hand in his.

"We're going to have a baby, John. The words still seem unreal, but I'm going to savour every one of them," Kathleen replied, her eyes sparkling with joy.

John's features relaxed, his smile warm and genuine. "You know, sweetheart, there are two things in life that change you forever: One is grief, and one is love."

Kathleen pondered John's words for a moment, then smiled softly. "I can't imagine going through this awful, wonderful life without you, my dearest. And now we have a whole new chapter to live, hand in hand."

"The best way forward that I know," John said, lifting his glass in a silent toast to Kathleen. "And we'll call him Robert, after your father," he teased.

"I think we'll call her Jennifer. Jennie for short," Kathleen teased back.

WANT to follow Jennie and her family as they share generations of heartwarming stories from Sunrise Island? Start by bringing a taste of Sunrise Island into your kitchen with a recipe from Kathleen, the beloved matriarch of Cliffhouse Farm. As you journey through the series, you'll discover even more of Kathleen's cherished recipes.

# KATHLEEN'S APPLE PANCAKE RECIPE

If you've ever spent the night at Cliffhouse Farm, you'll know Kathleen's apple pancakes are a must. The key to these fluffy treats isn't just the baking powder—it's the syrup. Only real Canadian maple syrup will do, no exceptions.

1 1/3 cups all-purpose flour
3 tsp baking powder
1/2 tsp salt
3 tbs sugar
1 egg
1 cup milk
3 tbs melted butter or vegetable oil
1/4 tsp vanilla
1 cup grated raw apple
1/2 tsp baking soda
1 tsp warm water

Stir flour, baking powder, salt, and sugar together. Beat egg thoroughly. Add milk.

Make a well in centre of dry ingredients. Slowly add egg-milk mixture. Add melted butter, vanilla, and grated apple plus the baking soda dissolved in warm water.

Stir quickly until ingredients are just mixed and batter is still lumpy.

Drop by 1/4 cupfuls on hot pancake griddle (375°F /190°C). Cook for 4-5 minutes or until pancakes are filled with bubbles and the underside is golden brown. Turn and brown the other side. (Do not turn more than once.)

Serve hot with real Canadian maple syrup.

# ABOUT THE AUTHOR

<u>Maren Hill</u>

Captivated by the intrigue of everyday life, Maren Hill writes heartfelt, emotional stories that celebrate women and the relationships that shape their lives.

Quirky, good-hearted characters you'd love to know and stories laced with romance, humour, compassion, and inspiration are trademarks of Maren Hill's books.

<u>J.D. Monk</u>

Did you know that this author wrote a best-selling children's book? *Slimy Slick* appeals to children and adults with fascinating facts about banana slugs.

If you enjoy my books, <u>please leave a review.</u> There's nothing more motivational than positive reviews. Thank you so much.

# ALSO BY MAREN HILL

Cliffhouse Footprints

Cliffhouse by the Sea

Sunrise Island Sisters

Sunrise Island Christmas

Sunrise Island Celebrations

Nicole

The Troublemakers

Our Forever Place

Make a Spectacular Seashell Lamp

Sealed with a Kiss

# WHAT READERS SAY

"Maren Hill's description of the island is so real that you can smell the salt air, feel the sand between your toes, the sun sparkling on the water, and hear the waves. Maren Hill weaves her stories extremely well."

"... she has a real knack for transporting the reader to the world of the story."

"The characters are great and the story is ... captivating."

"Awesome. Great setting, and relatable characters with solid backgrounds. Well written... character portrayal is solid with depth."

"... a suspenseful and mysterious story... will keep you on the edge of your seat."

"Excellent knack for transporting the reader into the world of the story... I can't wait for more. A true gem!"

"I thoroughly enjoyed ... Cliffhouse by the Sea... kept me wanting to know what would happen next."

"Maren Hill has done it again! Love this book. Would definitely read more by her."

"This story with Alexa and Kyla was riveting. I really enjoyed the dynamics of these two sisters. This is a great story."

"Beautifully done and exceptionally entertaining, heart-wrenching and delightful.

"Gorgeous writing! I love the author's rich descriptions of characters, scenes and situations - I felt like I was living it."

"JD Monk writes with a simplicity that pulls kids into the story immediately, but also with an underlying complexity and intelligence that allows the ideas in Slimy Slick to stay with them long after the tale ends. Well done!"

"This is a great story. Congratulations to the author for bringing awareness to these little creatures who are often misunderstood and undervalued. I love the education/entertainment combo. The illustrations are engaging and hilarious."

"Beautifully written and illustrated -- this is a wonderful bedtime story! Not only do we learn about the importance of banana slugs in our ecosystem in this story, but we're introduced to lovely language to increase the richness of our vocabulary. This is an awesome gift for children (and their parents) who are curious about their environment!"

"What a wonderful read! It was extremely informative about Banana Slugs; a very misunderstood creature. I learned a lot! The graphics are very well done! Definitely a must buy this Holiday Season for the little ones in the family!"

"Loved this book! Very well written, easy to understand and follow for children! Super informative as well, I had no idea slugs were this unique!"

"I have a whole new appreciation for slugs...The kids love it."

"... full of amazing facts about slugs... Completely recommend for curious kids who love nature."

"The fun facts were marvelous and very informative. 5 stars to the author. Highly recommend."

"Great book, full of lots of interesting slug facts. I recommend this for all young and young-at-heart bug lovers."

"Perfect for storytime and a wonderful way to explore nature!"

# SLIMY SLICK—NOT JUST FOR KIDS!

## The Nighttime Adventures of a Banana Slug

This captivating picture book appeals to kids and adults through multiple reads and is jam-packed with suspense, slime, and fun facts.

Join Slimy Slick on his exciting nighttime adventure through the countryside as he glides toward the tasty treat of his dreams. He encounters an earthworm and a shrew, but the real danger lies ahead. Will Slick's journey come to an abrupt end at the hands of a well-meaning boy whose mission is to capture and eliminate? Does he not understand Slick's important role in the ecosystem?

Readers learn about the clever design of the banana slug and how Slick uses his natural gifts to protect himself and navigate life in the wild.

Discover the world of Slimy Slick through a rainforest adventure that educates and entertains, emphasizing the importance of these fascinating creatures to our planet.

Perfect for:

• Parents and grandparents, science teachers, librarians, educators

• Gifts for kids who love nature, rainforest animals, and learning more about the natural world and zoology

• Read-aloud family sharing

• Gaining environmental wisdom

• Understanding empathy and collaboration

# ACKNOWLEDGEMENTS

Writing this novel has been a journey of the heart, and I am deeply grateful to those who have shaped my understanding of family. My parents, children, and grandchildren have been my greatest inspiration, influencing the very themes woven into these pages.

To my loved ones—thank you for your unwavering encouragement, support, and the countless ways you enrich my life. This story is a reflection of the love and lessons you have given me.